Dear Parent:

Congratulations! Your child is taking the first steps on an exciting journey. The destination? Independent reading!

STEP INTO READING® will help your child get there. The program offers five steps to reading success. Each step includes fun stories and colorful art. There are also Step into Reading Sticker Books, Step into Reading Math Readers, Step into Reading Write-In Readers, Step into Reading Phonics Readers, and Step into Reading Phonics First Steps! Boxed Sets—a complete literacy program with something for every child.

Learning to Read, Step by Step!

Ready to Read Preschool–Kindergarten
• big type and easy words • rhyme and rhythm • picture clues
For children who know the alphabet and are eager to begin reading.

Reading with Help Preschool–Grade 1
• basic vocabulary • short sentences • simple stories
For children who recognize familiar words and sound out new words with help.

Reading on Your Own Grades 1–3
• engaging characters • easy-to-follow plots • popular topics
For children who are ready to read on their own.

Reading Paragraphs Grades 2–3
• challenging vocabulary • short paragraphs • exciting stories
For newly independent readers who read simple sentences with confidence.

Ready for Chapters Grades 2–4
• chapters • longer paragraphs • full-color art
For children who want to take the plunge into chapter books but still like colorful pictures.

STEP INTO READING® is designed to give every child a successful reading experience. The grade levels are only guides. Children can progress through the steps at their own speed, developing confidence in their reading, no matter what their grade.

Remember, a lifetime love of reading starts with a single step!

For Kevin, my love and my friend

 Published in the United States by Random House Children's Books, a division of Random House, Inc., New York, in conjunction with Disney Enterprises, Inc.
www.stepintoreading.com
www.randomhouse.com/kids/disney
Educators and librarians, for a variety of teaching tools, visit us at
www.randomhouse.com/teachers
Library of Congress Cataloging-in-Publication Data
Lagonegro, Melissa.
Old, new, red, blue! / by Melissa Lagonegro.
p. cm. – (Step into reading. Step 1 book)
Summary: Cars and trucks introduce simple concepts such as color and size.
ISBN-13: 978-0-7364-2410-3 (trade)
ISBN-10: 0-7364-2410-5 (trade)
ISBN-13: 978-0-7364-8050-5 (lib. bdg.)
ISBN-10: 0-7364-8050-1 (lib. bdg.)
[1. Vehicles—Fiction.] I. Cars (Motion picture) II. Title. III. Series.
PZ8.3.L1363Ol 2006
[E]—dc22
2005033396

Printed in the United States of America 30 29 28 First Edition

OLD, NEW, RED, BLUE!

By Melissa Lagonegro

Random House New York

Old truck.

New car.

Red truck.

Blue car.

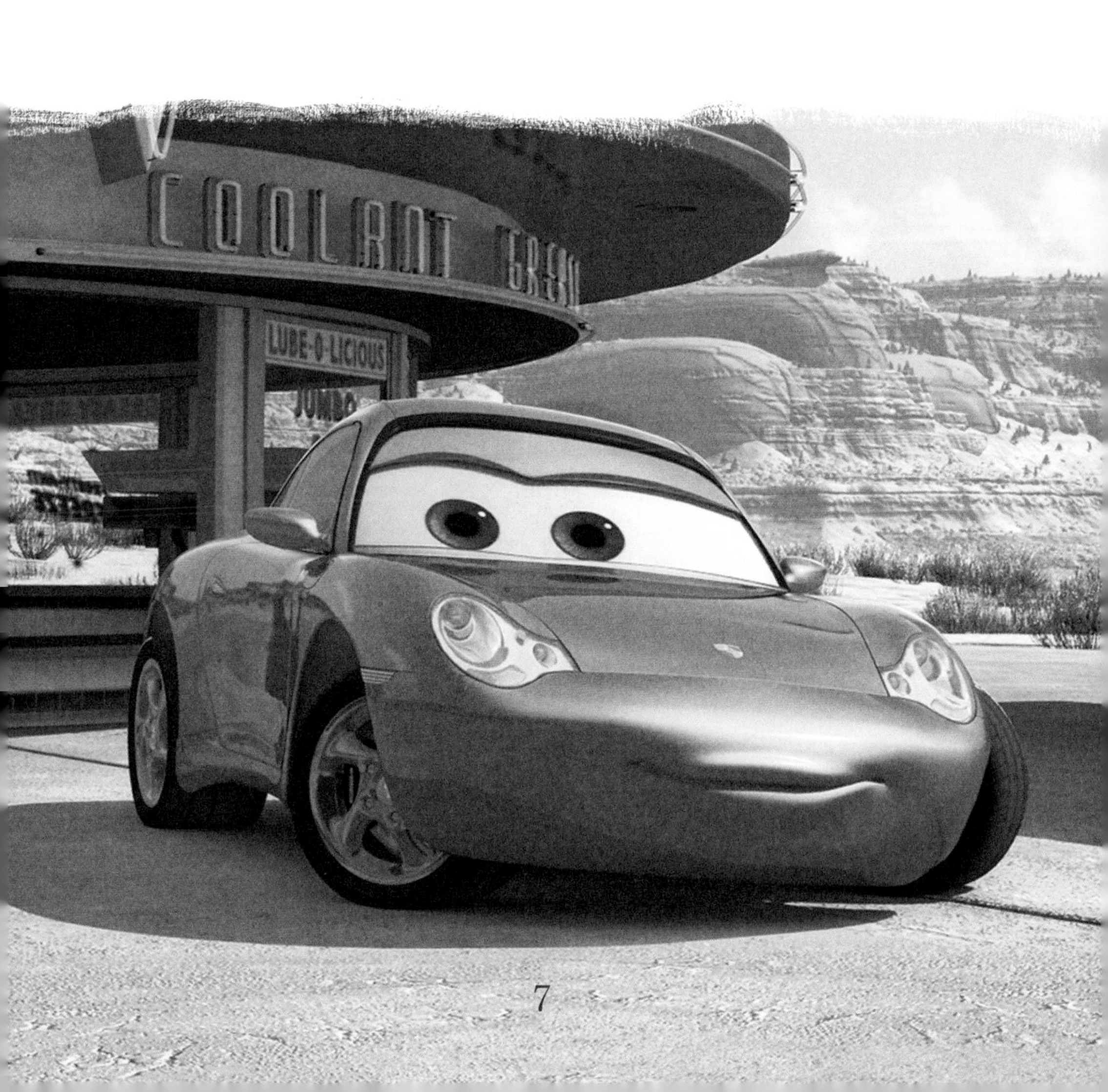

Shiny and bright.

CUP
LAP
208
43
43

Dull and brown.

Day on the highway.

Night in the town.

Dirty car.

RADIATOR SPRINGS
FIRE DEPARTMENT

Dirty car.

RADIATOR SPRINGS
FIRE DEPARTMENT

Clean car.

Nice car.

Mean car.

Drive fast, fast, fast.

Drive nice and slow.

Cars ride high.

Cars ride low.

Tires are big.
Tires are small.

Piles of tires,
short and tall.

Luigi's
CASA DELLA TIRES
Ferrari
Ferrari

Wheels rolling
on the ground.

Cars and trucks
drive all around.

Beep, beep!